CAROL NEVIUS

KARATE HOUR

Illustrated by
BILL THOMSON

MARSHALL CAVENDISH
NEW YORK LONDON SINGAPORE

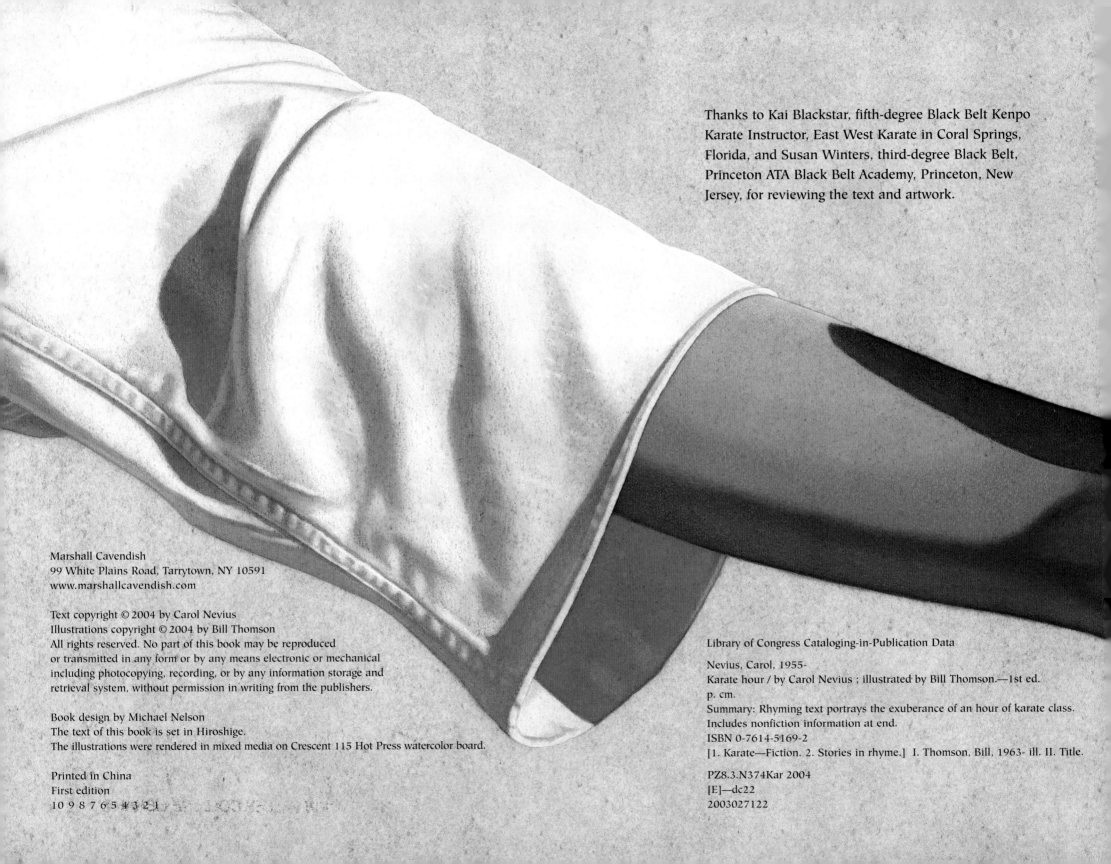

Thanks to Kai Blackstar, fifth-degree Black Belt Kenpo Karate Instructor, East West Karate in Coral Springs, Florida, and Susan Winters, third-degree Black Belt, Princeton ATA Black Belt Academy, Princeton, New Jersey, for reviewing the text and artwork.

Marshall Cavendish
99 White Plains Road, Tarrytown, NY 10591
www.marshallcavendish.com

Book design by Michael Nelson
The text of this book is set in Hiroshige.
The illustrations were rendered in mixed media on Crescent 115 Hot Press watercolor board.

Printed in China
First edition
10 9 8 7 6 5 4 3 2 1

Library of Congress Cataloging-in-Publication Data

Nevius, Carol, 1955-
Karate hour / by Carol Nevius ; illustrated by Bill Thomson.—1st ed.
p. cm.
Summary: Rhyming text portrays the exuberance of an hour of karate class.
Includes nonfiction information at end.
ISBN 0-7614-5169-2
[1. Karate—Fiction. 2. Stories in rhyme.] I. Thomson, Bill, 1963- ill. II. Title.

PZ8.3.N374Kar 2004
[E]—dc22
2003027122

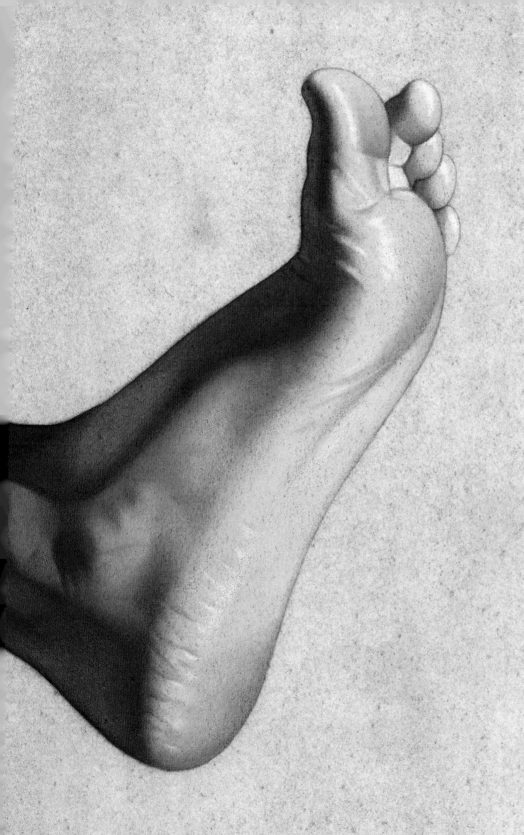

To all the patient karate instructors,
and to their striving students,
including Dylan, Nova, and Griffin
—C. N.

This book is dedicated to my dad, William S. Thomson.
Although our time together was far too short,
his love and influence will last a lifetime.
—B. T.

*K*arate hour is starting now.
Dressed and belted, we all bow.

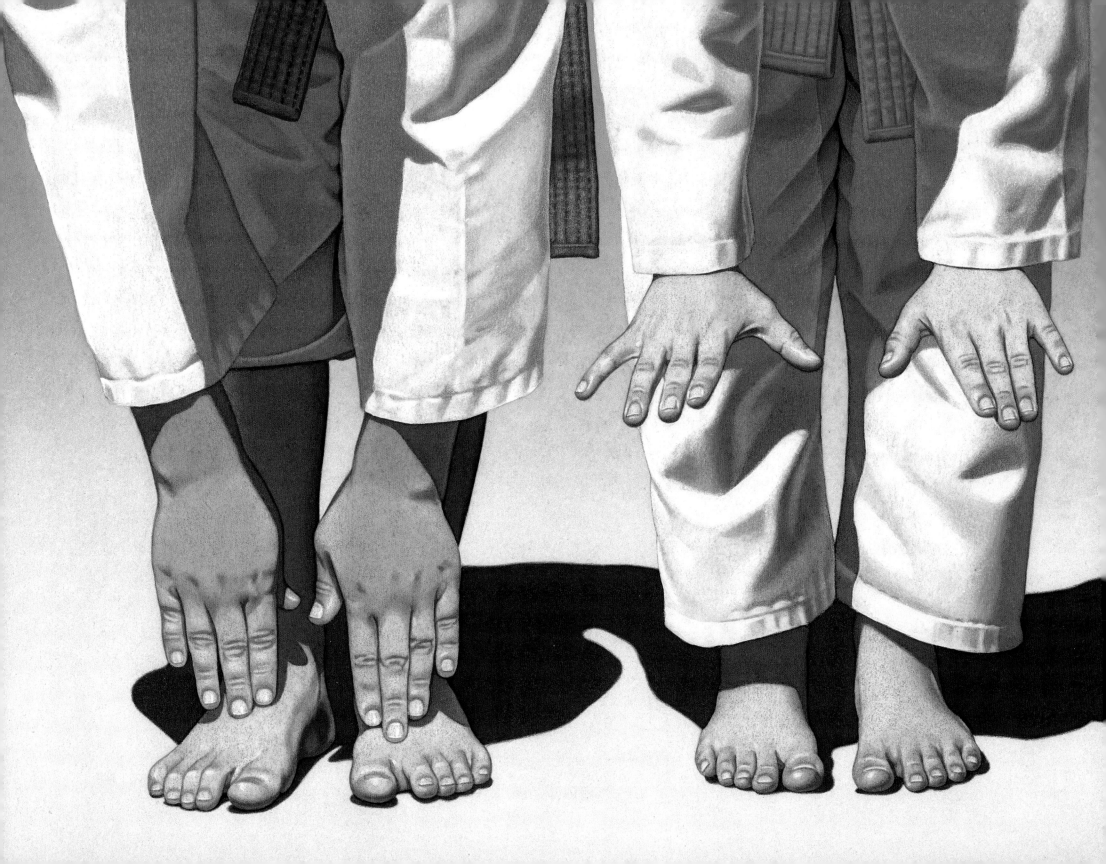

We show respect, walk to our place.
The master moves with strength and grace.
We space ourselves to stand in rows.
We reach and bend to touch our toes.

We stretch our legs, improve our split,
For crescent kicks and to be fit.

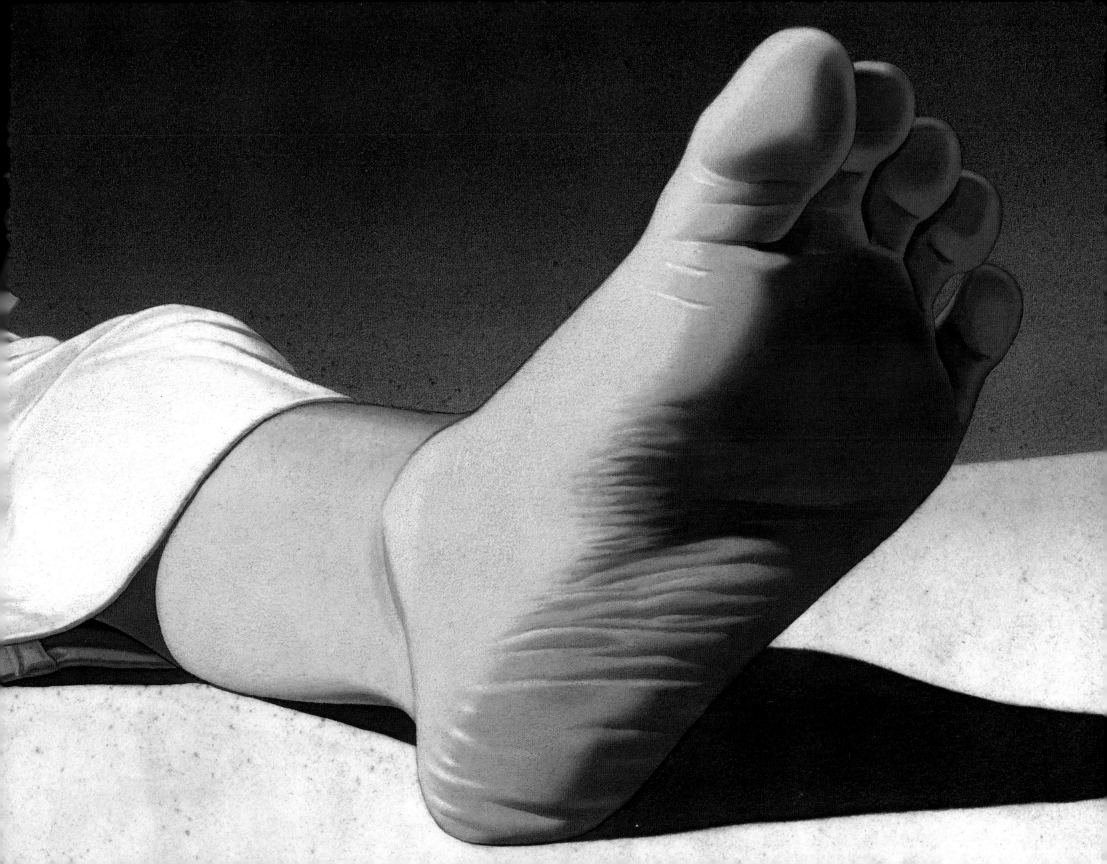

The master and his helper see
A snappy front kick from the knee.

We crouch into a low drop stance,
And check for danger with a glance.

We energize. Our muscles flex.
We raise our arms, protect our necks.
We yell "Hai-ya!" and feel our power,
Growing in karate hour.

We clench our fists, then straighten hands.
We jump and twist, do tuck-roll-stands.

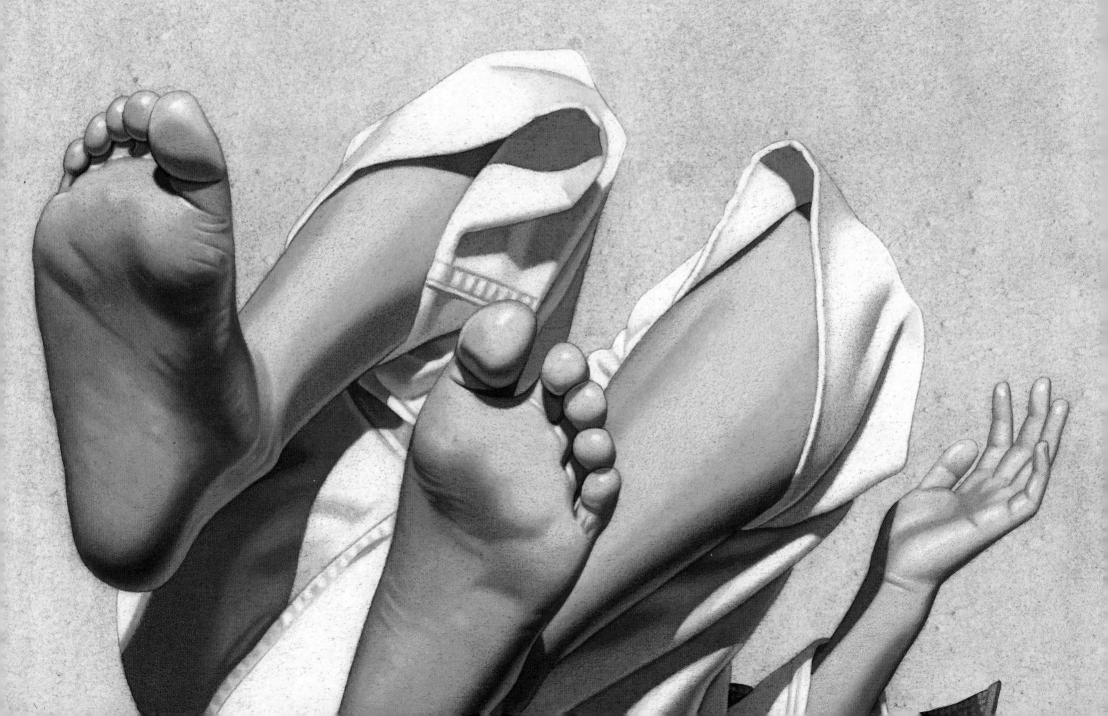

A barefoot kick can break a board,
The splintered wooden halves reward.

We run and leap, land on our feet,
With balance, moving to the beat.

The dark belts spar, "Ki-ai!" We learn.
We watch and wait to have a turn.

We kneel in line to chant our pact.
We'll use defense, and we'll react.
We'll practice using self-control,
With mind and body as a whole.
The color of our belts will show
Karate progress, skills we know.

We bow. High five! Head to the shower,
Feeling great—Karate Hour!

AUTHOR'S NOTE

No one knows exactly where karate, "the way of the open hand," originated. One legend tells of a fifth-century Indian Buddhist monk named Bohidharma who designed a set of exercises to strengthen the mind and body. He traveled to China, where his Zen teachings and disciplines took hold. These became the basis for temple boxing, and spread to Korea and Japan, developing into various martial arts over periods of thousands of years.

Whatever the origin, most people agree that karate as we know it today took shape in Okinawa, one of Japan's smaller islands. Because there were two long periods in which weapons were banned, the Okinawans developed self-defense and fighting techniques using only karate.

Wearing their nightclothes, the basis for today's *gi*, or training uniform, they practiced secretly at night. Over many years time, their belts changed color to indicate rank, and they earned the honored Japanese title of *sensei*, which means "one who has gone before, teacher, or master." Sensei Gichin Funakoshi is considered karate's founding father. He brought it from Okinawa and introduced it into mainland Japan in 1922.

Although karate developed in Okinawa, karate classes for fitness and self-defense can now be found in communities throughout the world. Stances, punches, blocks, and kicks, in various combinations called *katas*, have been perfected over time.

The sensei of the *dojo*, or training hall, teaches the kata movements and supervises all sparring, the practice of using one's martial-art skills to fight against another student of the same rank. This is done only in class. Opponents always show their respect with a bow, both before and after sparring. They use self-control so their kicks, blocks, and blows will do no harm. Lighter belts practice carefully rehearsed katas for self-defense and counterattack. Generally, only the older, more experienced, darker-belted students are allowed to free-spar. Younger, lighter belts are invited to sit and learn by watching. Many class hours, and at least three years of rigorous training, are needed to become a *shodan*, or first-degree black belt.

A commonly used saying is "There is no first attack in karate." Students start by learning stances and blocks to protect themselves. They are encouraged to use the Japanese words *Hai-ya*, which means "yes" and *Ki-ai*, a shout that expresses spiritual energy. This helps direct breathing and focuses force to one's actions; it sometimes scares away the enemy. Punches, thrusts, and kicks for counterattack are only for the purpose of stopping the opponent before the attack can advance further. *Karate aims to finish what someone else starts*, while also stressing the values of modesty, courtesy, integrity, and perseverance.

The gi consists of white, loose-fitting pants and a jacket that's tied and held closed by a long cloth belt. Beginners at the tenth *kyu* (the lowest rank) wear white belts. As they learn new katas, they may earn colored belts after being tested three or four times a year by the sensei.

Dan is the Japanese term for the upper ranks. *Shodan* is first-degree black belt; *nidan* is second; *sandan* is third. Dan levels theoretically can advance to ten. In some dojos the sensei may also choose to wear a black gi with the black belt. The rare ninth-or tenth-degree dan may wear a red belt. The exact kyu and belt color worn may differ from dojo to dojo, but the principle is universal: In karate as in other martial arts, darker belts indicate advanced skills.

HERE IS A TYPICAL RANKING ORDER:

10th kyu
WHITE BELT

9th and 8th kyus
YELLOW BELT

7th and 6th kyus
ORANGE BELT

5th kyu
GREEN BELT

4th kyu
PURPLE BELT

3rd, 2nd, and 1st kyus
BROWN BELT

1st to 8th dans
BLACK BELT

9th and 10th dans
RED BELT

DOJO KUN

(TRAINING HALL RULES)

SEEK PERFECTION OF CHARACTER

BE FAITHFUL

ENDEAVOR

RESPECT OTHERS

REFRAIN FROM VIOLENT BEHAVIOR

The rules shown here are an example of those recited at the end of every karate class. All are considered equally important. As with the belt colors, the exact phrasing of the rules may differ from dojo to dojo.